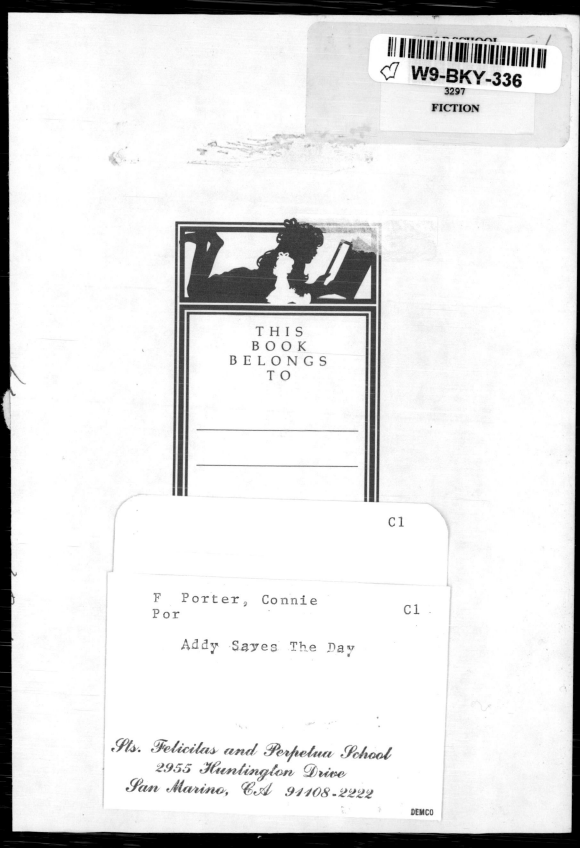

THIS
BOOK
BELONGS
TO

_____

_____

The Books About Addy

Meet Addy · An American Girl

Addy and her mother try to escape from slavery because
they hope to be free and to reunite their family.

❋

Addy Learns a Lesson · A School Story

Addy starts her life as a free person in Philadelphia. She
learns about reading and writing—and freedom.

❋

Addy's Surprise · A Christmas Story

Addy and Momma are generous with the little money
they've saved—and thrilled by a great surprise.

❋

Happy Birthday, Addy! · A Springtime Story

Addy makes a new friend, who encourages her to claim
a birthday and helps her face prejudice.

❋

Addy Saves the Day · A Summer Story

The Civil War is over, but not the feud between Addy and
Harriet, until tragedy forces them to come together at last.

❋

Changes for Addy · A Winter Story

The long struggle to reunite Addy's family finally ends, but
there is heartache along with the happiness.

ADDY
SAVES
THE DAY
A SUMMER STORY

BY CONNIE PORTER

ILLUSTRATIONS BRADFORD BROWN

VIGNETTES RENÉE GRAEF, GERI STRIGENZ BOURGET

PLEASANT COMPANY

Published by Pleasant Company Publications Incorporated
© Copyright 1994 by Pleasant Company Incorporated
All rights reserved. No part of this book may be used or reproduced in
any manner whatsoever without written permission except in the case of
brief quotations embodied in critical articles and reviews.
For information, address: Book Editor,
Pleasant Company Publications Incorporated,
8400 Fairway Place, P.O. Box 620998,
Middleton, WI 53562.

First Edition.
Printed in the United States of America.
94 95 96 97 98 99 RND 10 9 8 7 6 5 4 3 2 1

The American Girls Collection® and Addy Walker™
are trademarks of Pleasant Company.

PICTURE CREDITS
The following individuals and organizations have generously given permission to reprint
illustrations contained in "Looking Back": pp. 62-63—Museum of the City of New York
(Central Park); Courtesy: International Harvester Company (factory); New-York Historical
Society (children playing); pp. 64-65—New-York Historical Society (Central Park); Courtesy,
City of Claremont, N.H., photo, Index of American Sculpture, University of Delaware (New
Hampshire Memorial); Saint-Gaudens National Historic Site (Boston memorial); pp. 66-67—
American (New Castle, DE) Bathing Suit, c. 1855, Philadelphia Museum of Art; New-York
Historical Society (children playing baseball); Transcendental Graphics (baseball); Library of
Congress (family).

Edited by Roberta Johnson
Designed by Myland McRevey and Jane S. Varda
Art Directed by Kathleen A. Brown

Library of Congress Cataloging-in-Publication Data

Porter, Connie Rose, 1959-
Addy saves the day : a summer story / by Connie Porter ; illustrations, Bradford Brown ;
vignettes, Renée Graef, Geri Strigenz Bourget. — 1st ed.
p. cm. — (The American girls collection)
Summary: Addy and Harriet feud over everything, including fund-raising plans to help the
families of freed slaves, but tragedy finally forces them to stop fighting and work together.

ISBN 1-56247-084-1 — ISBN 1-56247-083-3 (pbk.)
[1. Afro-Americans—Fiction. 2. Conduct of life—Fiction. 3. Friendship—Fiction.
4. Slavery—Fiction.] I. Brown, Bradford, ill. II. Title. III. Series.
PZ7.P825Add   1994   [Fic]—dc20   94-11267   CIP   AC

TO MY NIECES
AND NEPHEWS

TABLE OF CONTENTS

ADDY'S FAMILY
AND FRIENDS

ADDY'S FAMILY

POPPA
Addy's father, whose dream gives the family strength.

MOMMA
Addy's mother, whose love helps the family survive.

ADDY
A courageous girl, smart and strong, growing up during the Civil War.

SAM
Addy's sixteen-year-old brother, determined to be free.

ESTHER
Addy's two-year-old sister.

. . . AND FRIENDS

SARAH MOORE
Addy's good friend.

REVEREND DRAKE
*The inspiring
minister at Trinity
A.M.E. Church.*

MRS. DRAKE
*The leader of the
children's group at
Trinity A.M.E. Church.*

HARRIET DAVIS
*Addy's snobby desk
partner at school.*

SEEDS OF HOPE

Addy Walker stood in the middle of the garden with her eyes closed and her face tilted up to the late afternoon sun. She loved the feel of its warmth on her face.

Poppa called to Addy, "What you doing? Resting? You supposed to be breaking up the ground so we can plant some seeds."

Addy smiled at Poppa. "I'm trying," she said. "But it's hard, Poppa."

"Of course it's hard," said Momma, who was working with a pitchfork. "Nothing good come easy."

"I don't mean that kind of hard," said Addy. "I mean the ground real hard. I can't get my hoe to break through it."

"Let me help you," Poppa said.

Addy, Momma, and Poppa were working in a large garden about a mile from their boarding house. There wasn't enough room at the boarding house for a garden, so they had rented a small plot and were planting some vegetables and a few flowers. Other people had rented plots in the large garden, too.

Addy watched as Poppa easily broke through the surface of the ground with his shovel. The dirt on top was a lighter color than the dirt deeper down. Poppa picked up a big clump of earth that was as dark as coffee.

"Look how rich this earth is," Poppa said. "We gonna harvest a heap of vegetables."

Addy wiggled her bare toes in the earth Poppa had turned over. It was cool and soft. "I wish we could plant some fruit, too," she said. "I sure would like some berries."

"Well, we'll see," replied Poppa. "Remember, we ain't planting this garden for ourselves. We doing it to raise money."

"I know," Addy said. The money they would make from selling their vegetables would help them in their search for her baby sister Esther and her

*"Remember," said Poppa, "we ain't planting this garden
for ourselves. We doing it to raise money."*

older brother Sam. In the two months since the Civil War had ended, Addy, Poppa, and Momma had tried hard to reunite their family. They had taken letters to aid societies, written to the Freedman's Bureau, and placed an ad in *The Christian Recorder* newspaper. They had even sent a letter to Master Stevens's plantation, where they had been slaves, hoping someone would read it to Auntie Lula and Uncle Solomon. But they had not received any answers or any news about Esther or Sam. Now Poppa was determined to go back to the plantation as soon as he could to get Esther and to find out where Sam might be. Poppa would need money for his trip.

Addy followed behind Poppa, using her hoe to chop up the big chunks of earth he turned over. Every time she struck one of the chunks, her hands stung from the wooden handle rubbing against her skin. Sometimes she hit rocks hidden under the dirt, and she felt the hoe bounce and jiggle in her hands. She dug out the rocks and loaded them into the wheelbarrow to get them out of the way.

Clearing out a thick patch of weeds

in the middle of the plot was the toughest work of all. The weeds came up as high as Addy's knees. Some of them had burrs that snagged her dress and dug into her skin. The weeds were stubborn, and Addy had to use all her strength to yank them out of the ground. Soon her back ached from bending over, and sweat ran down her face.

"Let's stop and rest a bit," Momma said. She paused a moment to wipe sweat from her brow. "We can sit down and have our picnic supper."

Momma had packed up their dinner from the boarding house and brought it to the garden. Addy was happy to think about supper—and resting. Resting wasn't allowed back on the plantation. Addy shuddered, remembering her life when she was a slave. When she worked in the tobacco fields then, the overseer watched the slaves with a whip in his hand. They couldn't stop when they were tired or have a drink of water unless the overseer said they could.

But it was different now. Momma spread an old blanket on the ground. As they ate and drank, Addy said, "If you had the chance to ask God a question, what would you ask?"

"That's easy for me," answered Momma. "I would ask what we have to do to get our family together again. I'd ask how we can get Esther, Sam, Auntie Lula, and Uncle Solomon here, safe in Philadelphia with us."

Addy turned to Poppa. "What about you, Poppa?"

"I don't know, but I might ask how I got a daughter that ask so many questions," Poppa said. He let out a loud chuckle.

Momma and Addy laughed, too. Then Addy said seriously, "I'd ask why there had to be slavery."

"There didn't *have* to be slavery," Momma said. "People chose to have it. Folks do plenty of things they know is wrong."

"If it wasn't for slavery, our whole family would be together," Addy said fiercely. "That's why I hate Master Stevens."

"You know I don't like you talking that way," Momma scolded gently.

"But I *do* hate him," Addy insisted. "Everything is his fault. He sold Poppa and Sam away from us. Then you and I had to run away from him and leave Esther behind with Auntie Lula and Uncle Solomon."

Poppa spoke to Addy with understanding.
"What you feeling right now is a lot of bitterness,"
he said. "I know, because I feel the same way
sometimes. It's hard not to." He sighed.
Then he went on to say, "But you got to
know, Addy, anger and bitterness can
be like weeds. If you let them grow,
pretty soon they take over and there
ain't room for nothing else."

Momma poured more water into Addy's
drinking gourd. "I feel angry, too, sometimes," she
said. "But I feel other things even stronger. I want
to hold Esther in my arms and give Sam a big hug.
I want to spend evenings talking to Auntie Lula and
Uncle Solomon. I want . . ." Momma stopped talking
and stared off into the distance.

Addy moved closer to Momma. She knew how
sad Momma was and how much she missed the rest
of the family. Touching the cowrie shell on her
necklace, Addy remembered what Momma had told
her. This shell was a reminder to hold on to love for
her family, even when she was far away from them.

"I want us all to be back together, too," Addy
said softly.

Poppa stood up and held out his hand to help Momma stand up, too. "Let's clear out the rest of these weeds," he said. "Then we can start planting."

Addy worked steadily alongside Momma and Poppa for another hour, stopping only to rub dirt on her hands to keep the handle of the hoe from slipping so much. When they finished weeding, Poppa stretched long pieces of string from one end of the plot to the other to help lay out straight rows. Then he walked along one of the strings and used the hoe to make a furrow in the dirt.

When they started planting, Addy knelt between Momma and Poppa. She watched their hands carefully. Gently, they dropped seeds into the furrow and then, even more gently, they smoothed dirt over the seeds.

Addy tried to be as careful as Momma and Poppa. The seeds were precious—not just because they cost money, but because the plants that grew from these seeds would help her family be reunited. Addy knew she was planting seeds of hope.

It took a long time to plant the seeds, and Addy was tired when she finally walked to the stream to wash her sore hands in the water. But it was the good tiredness that comes from doing an important job.

"Poppa," Addy said. "Tomorrow is Saturday. I don't have school. Can I come work in the garden while you and Momma are at work?"

"Momma and I got the day off tomorrow," said Poppa, washing the dirt from his hands. "None of us gonna go to work tomorrow—in the garden or anyplace else. Don't you remember, Addy? Tomorrow the day of the big parade, the Grand Review."

"But that parade gonna have only white soldiers marching in it," said Addy. "Why we got to go see them march?"

"Because their fighting helped bring slavery to an end, that's why," Momma said. "And we should honor them for being brave."

"Well, I hope when the colored soldiers come home they have a parade for them," said Addy. "They was brave, too. If Sam ever got to be a soldier, I'm sure he was real brave."

"I got no doubt about that," Poppa said. "I ain't never known your brother to be scared of a thing. Sam is something special."

"He brave and smart and funny," said Addy.

"Remember how he was always riddling me? 'Riddle me this,' he'd say. 'What's smaller than a dog, but can put a bear on the run?'"

Poppa laughed. "I got a riddle for you now," he said as he gathered up the garden tools. "What's big and red and sinking fast? The sun! We better get back to the boarding house."

"Can't I stay a little longer?" asked Addy. "I want to water the seeds I planted."

"All right," said Poppa. "But come straight home soon as you finish."

"I will," promised Addy. She filled up her watering can at the stream as Momma and Poppa left. Then she walked slowly up and down the rows, giving the newly planted seeds a generous drink of water. Addy felt pleased as she watered the garden. Her hands were still burning a little, but she didn't mind. The seeds they had planted lay safe under the blanket of rich soil, and soon, with help, they would grow.

"Well, well, well, if it isn't the little plantation girl," said a sharp voice behind Addy.

Addy whirled around to see Harriet standing

10

at the edge of the plot, smirking at her. Harriet was a girl from her school whom she did not like.

"You look right at home in that dirt patch," Harriet went on.

"It ain't a dirt patch," Addy said. "It's a garden, a vegetable garden."

"Vegetables?" asked Harriet. "What's the matter? Don't your parents make enough money to buy food for you to eat?"

"We gonna sell the vegetables," said Addy proudly. "My poppa gonna use the money to go back to the plantation to get my sister and look for my brother."

"Oh, yes," said Harriet. "You told me about your lost brother. He's the one you think *might* have been a soldier." She smiled a superior smile. "My uncle served with distinction in the Third Infantry. He'll be home any day now. My mother says she expects he is a hero and will have the medals to prove it. We're going to have a big party for him."

"My brother Sam coming home, too, someday," said Addy stubbornly. "I'm sure of it."

Harriet shrugged to show that she did not care. "Well, I shouldn't keep you from your dirt patch—

I mean, your *garden*," she said. And she flounced away.

Addy watched her go, feeling hurt and angry and jealous. If only she knew as much about Sam as Harriet knew about her uncle! Addy gathered her hoe and her watering can and headed home. The sun had fallen behind the buildings and the evening air was cold.

When Addy got back to the boarding house, she washed her hands carefully. Momma had set out a sheet of paper, a pen, and an inkwell on the table for Addy to write another letter about Esther and Sam.

Addy knew the supplies cost precious money. She didn't want to make any mistakes when she wrote because that would be wasteful. Momma and Poppa sat next to Addy at the table and reminded her of what she should say.

"You got to remember to say where we last saw everybody," Momma said.

"That's right," said Poppa. "And make sure you tell how they can find us here in Philadelphia."

"And don't forget to say we love them all," Momma reminded Addy.

Addy smiled. "I won't leave that part out," she said as she dipped her pen in the ink and carefully began writing. Momma and Poppa watched as she wrote, their faces full of concern.

Scritch, scratch. Addy moved the pen across the paper. She knew the words she wrote were nothing more than shapes to Poppa, who could not read or write. When she finished, she read the letter to her parents.

"That's real nice, Addy," Momma said.

Poppa nodded. "You write real good," he said. "We'll take the letter to the Quaker Aid Society first thing in the morning, before the parade."

June 9, 1865

Dear Friends,

Can you help us find our family? Please. Solomon and Lula Morgan. They caring for our dear baby Esther Walker. We last seen them last summer on the plantation belonging to Master Stevens. The plantation is some twenty miles north of Raleigh. We need information about Samuel Walker also. He about 17 years old. He was sold from the Stevens plantation last summer. We don't know where he was sold to. If you can help us, write to Ben Walker on South Street in Philadelphia, Penn. We want to find them very much because we love them all.

Ben Walker

Addy held the letter in her hands for a moment. She thought about Harriet's knowing where her uncle was. Harriet could send her uncle a letter anytime she wanted to. *This letter got to get to somebody who knows something about Esther and Sam,* Addy thought. *It's just got to.* Then she folded the letter carefully. She hoped the letter, like the seeds she'd planted in the garden, would help her family be together again.

HOPE AND DETERMINATION

 Saturday morning dawned bright and blue. Addy felt hopeful as she walked along between Momma and Poppa. They were all dressed in their Sunday best in honor of the Grand Review. Before they went to the parade, they were going to the Quaker meeting hall to deliver their letter. Outside the meeting hall, Poppa took off his hat and checked to be sure the letter was safe in his coat pocket. They went inside and walked to a small room in the back of the hall where the Quaker Aid Society had its office.

"Good morning!" a pleasant voice called to them. It was Mr. Cooper, who had helped them on other visits, his face beaming with a smile. Addy smiled back at him. She liked Mr. Cooper. He was a little man with thick, curly blond hair and a kind manner.

"It's good to see you all again," Mr. Cooper said. "How are you?"

"We just fine," answered Momma. "We hoping for some good news about our family."

"Did anybody answer our last letter?" Addy asked brightly.

"I'm afraid not," Mr. Cooper said. "But these things take time, you know."

"We been finding that out," Poppa said. "This waiting and not knowing is trying my patience."

Mr. Cooper looked sorry. "It breaks my heart knowing so many families are divided," he said. "I wish I could do more to help. Just this week, thirty people have come looking for help finding their families. I know some of them will never be reunited." Mr. Cooper shook his head. "Yesterday a young man stopped by who has been coming here for months trying to find his mother. Just the day before, I had gotten word that his mother passed away, and I had to tell him that."

Addy felt her throat tighten. She didn't want to

think about her family getting news as bad as that.

She was glad to hear Poppa say in a sure voice, "I tell you what, Mr. Cooper. My family can't give up hoping. Hope is all we got."

"Hope and determination," said Mr. Cooper. He took the letter from Poppa and smiled at Addy. "That's two good things you got working for you, Mr. Walker."

From the Quaker meeting hall it was a short walk to the parade route. Addy and her parents joined thousands of people already lining the street under banners that swooped from building to building. Addy had never seen such huge American flags or so much red, white, and blue bunting. It seemed to her that there were more people in the streets now than there had been the night the war ended. The sidewalks were so crowded that some boys had climbed to the top of light poles to get a good view of the parade.

The sounds of clashing cymbals, booming drums, and brassy horns burst through the air. Addy liked the way the music sounded, so strong and proud. Though she could hear the music, she couldn't see the musicians or the marching soldiers. She stood on tiptoe, trying to see over the people, but the crowd formed a wall taller than she was.

"I can't see nothing, Poppa," she complained.

"I can fix that," said Poppa. He lifted Addy and sat her on his shoulders. "What about now?" Poppa asked.

"I can see everything," Addy exclaimed. "This is the best seat!"

A band was just passing by. The musicians wore blue uniforms with gleaming brass buttons. Now Addy could see the soldiers, too. Hundreds and hundreds of them marched by in straight lines. Some of the soldiers rode horses. Addy smiled to see that even the horses looked special for the occasion. They pranced past with their manes braided and their thick tails well brushed. As far as Addy could see, the blue of the soldiers' uniforms filled the street. The soldiers carried rifles, and many had shining swords hanging from their belts. Addy looked at their faces. She was surprised  to see how young some of the soldiers were. They looked younger than Sam.

A red-haired woman stood next to Momma and

Poppa, waving a small flag. She turned to them and said, "Look! There's my son. That's Jimmy! He's the one with red hair in the front row."

"He's a fine-looking boy," Momma replied.

"You must be very proud of your son," Poppa added.

The woman wiped tears from her face as her son marched past.

"I'm so glad Jimmy made it home," she said. "My other son was killed in a battle in Virginia. Do you know what it's like to have your child die in a place you've never seen—and you never have the chance to say good-bye?"

"We can understand your feelings," Poppa said kindly. "There ain't no greater pain than losing a child."

The woman's story made Addy think of Sam. He had wanted so badly to be a soldier. Had he become one? Would he ever come marching home, proud and tall like these soldiers? As Addy watched the blue sea of troops flowing down the street, she felt tears fill her eyes. If Sam *had* managed to escape from slavery and become a soldier, he could be dead and they wouldn't even know it. She felt another stab of envy for Harriet. Addy tried to put the worried and jealous thoughts out of her mind, but they were like stubborn weeds that refused to be uprooted.

☀

The next morning, Addy sat between Momma and her friend Sarah in the women's section of Trinity A.M.E. Church. Sunlight poured through the stained-glass windows, filling the church with red, green, purple, and golden beams of light. She couldn't wait for Reverend Drake to finish his sermon. After church, she and her parents were going to work in the garden. Addy squirmed with impatience.

Momma put her arm around Addy and whispered, "Be still now, honey."

Addy stopped squirming. She settled back in the pew, close to Sarah, and gazed at the beautiful rays of light while Reverend Drake spoke. When he finished his sermon, Addy thought it was time to leave. But then Reverend Drake started to make an announcement.

"I know for many of you, the war isn't over yet," Reverend Drake began. "Many of you still aren't at peace, and how can you be? The country was torn apart by the Civil War. Just after it finally ended, President Lincoln was killed. He gave his life trying to make the country one again, North and South. The war has torn your families apart. Many families are scattered, your children lost, your fathers and sons, uncles and brothers still not home with you. Many of you begin every day with a prayer to see your loved ones again, and end the day with the same prayer."

Addy sat up straight and listened hard. It seemed as if Reverend Drake was speaking directly to her.

"Some of you pray for healing. Maybe you have a loved one who was wounded in the war or is sick and in the hospital fighting for his life. You pray as hard as you can. God hears your prayers. He knows what hopes you have in your hearts. You know He answers prayers."

"Amen!" Addy heard several voices call out.

"That's right," Reverend Drake went on, "and you also know that God helps those who help themselves. That's why I'm asking for your help this morning."

Addy leaned forward to hear what Reverend Drake was going to say.

"Our church is going to put on a fair the second Saturday in July. We're going to work hard, all of us together, to raise money. The money will help hospitals crowded with men who were wounded in the war. It will help families who were separated find each other again. The money will help organizations that are taking care of the widows and orphans left alone by the war. Members of other churches will join us in putting on the fair so we can earn money for these important causes.

"Now I am asking each and every one of you to join in this fund-raising effort and work hard. Come to a meeting here at the church next Thursday to make plans. Will you be here?"

"Amen, Reverend!" shouted several people.

Addy squeezed Momma's hand and looked up into her face. Momma smiled back, and Addy knew that she and Momma were thinking the same thing. The fair would help families just like theirs. They would work hard to make it a success.

※

When Thursday night came, Addy, Momma, and Poppa were among the first to arrive at church for the meeting about the fair. The grown-ups were meeting on the first floor. When Addy went down stairs to the Sabbath school room for the children's meeting, Sarah was already there.

"Hey, Addy!" Sarah called out. "I saved you a seat."

Addy and Sarah talked while they waited for the other children to arrive. When the group from First Baptist Church came in, Addy couldn't believe her eyes. Harriet was leading the way!

"Look who's here," Sarah said.

"Oh, no," Addy said as she slumped down on her bench. "Working with her is gonna be as much fun as having a toothache."

Mrs. Drake was the leader of their group. She offered all the children molasses cookies and iced tea. Addy and Sarah sat next to each other, munching on their cookies. Addy looked over at Harriet, but Harriet acted as if she didn't know her.

24

"Children," said Mrs. Drake, calling the meeting to order. "We are here to decide on a project you can do to raise money at the fair. Now, I think—"

Harriet interrupted in a loud voice, "I know what we should do!"

Sarah nudged Addy. "Here we go," she whispered. "Bossy Harriet!"

Mrs. Drake finished her sentence. "Now, I think it will work best if you raise your hand before you speak," she said, with a glance at Harriet.

Harriet slowly raised her hand, but a boy from First Baptist shot his arm in the air, and Mrs. Drake called on him first.

The boy said, "We could have a pie-eating contest. Our church had one for a fall festival, and it was fun."

"But messy!" said another boy with a laugh. "Why don't we sell toy boats instead?"

Harriet raised her hand higher, and Mrs. Drake called on her. "Those ideas are not as good as mine," Harriet said. "I think we should present a magic show. I will be the magician. I can pull rabbits out of hats and make things disappear."

"I wish *she* would disappear," Sarah whispered to Addy.

Addy hid a giggle behind her hand. She thought hard while Harriet talked on about the magic show, telling the group how much they should charge for tickets, how many tickets they'd sell, and how much money they would make.

"Well, Harriet," interrupted Mrs. Drake. "Thank you! You certainly are fast at adding up figures. But does anyone else have suggestions for a project?"

Addy raised her hand and spoke. "We could make spool puppets," she said. "My poppa showed me how to make them. They real easy, and I could get free spools from the dress shop where my momma work."

"Sound good," said Sarah.

"I think so, too," said the boy who had suggested the pie-eating contest.

All the other children liked Addy's idea, too, except Harriet. "Puppets! How boring!" she said. "A magic show would be much better and much more fun."

"Spool puppets is lots of fun," said Addy. "You can make them move and dance around." Suddenly Addy had an inspiration. "I know! Maybe my poppa could even make a little stage, and we could put on

*"We could make spool puppets," Addy said. "My poppa
showed me how to make them."*

a puppet show at the fair. We could tell jokes and riddles. Then everybody would see how much fun puppets is and they'd buy them."

"I think that's a splendid idea!" Mrs. Drake said. "How many of you agree?"

Everyone's hand went up—except Harriet's.

"Well, then," said Mrs. Drake, "I think we've decided. We'll make spool puppets and put on a show with them. Let's meet here a week from today to start making our puppets."

The children agreed and stood up to leave.

Addy caught Harriet's eye and smiled smugly. Harriet made a face, but Addy didn't care. Her idea had won over Harriet's.

On the way home from the meeting, Addy held Momma's hand and listened while Momma and Poppa talked about the projects the grown-ups were going to do for the fair.

"The women had a real nice meeting," said Momma. "We gonna bake pies to sell and make quilts to raffle. I said I'd bring some seedlings from the garden. All the women thought they'd sell well."

"That sound good," said Poppa. "The men gonna build all the booths for the fair. Deacon Martin got a

peanut wagon, and he said he'll supply tree
roasted peanuts for us to sell. I said I'd
make slide whistles for you kids to
sell." Poppa turned to Addy.
"What's your group doing,
honey?" he asked. "Since we left

slide whistle

church, you been bubbling over like a pot of hot
milk. I know you got something you want to tell."

Addy smiled. "We had the best meeting. We
making spool puppets." She turned to Momma.
"Can you get us empty spools from the shop?"

"I sure can," answered Momma.

"Good!" said Addy. "And Poppa, could you
build a puppet stage? We want to put on puppet
shows so people can see how the puppets move."

"I can do that," Poppa said.

"Thank you," said Addy. "The puppets and the
show were my idea. Everybody except that snotty
Harriet liked my idea. She was so jealous that my
idea beat hers! When she hear you're making slide
whistles too, Poppa, she gonna have another fit!"

Momma and Poppa were quiet. Then Poppa
said, "You disappointing me with that boastful
pride, Addy. You know the fair ain't a contest."

29

Addy felt a warm flush of shame spread over her face.

Momma said, "I know you and Harriet hit it off like a dog and cat, but you working together now. This is your chance to make peace with each other."

"I'm sorry I said what I did," Addy replied. "I'm gonna try harder to get along with Harriet, I promise."

Momma squeezed Addy's hand. "That's all we asking," Momma said.

☀

That night, after Addy got ready for bed, Poppa said, "Come here, Addy. Me and your momma need to talk to you about something."

Addy didn't like the tone of Poppa's voice. It sounded as if he might have some bad news to tell. He and Momma were sitting at the table. The lamp was lit, casting huge shadows in the room. Addy went over to them and asked in a worried voice, "What's wrong?"

"Nothing," Poppa said. "It's just that me and your momma changed our plans for me to go back to the plantation to get Esther. I don't have to wait until we sell our vegetables. Reverend Drake say the church gonna give me part of the money earned at the fair to help me on my trip. So I'm going in three weeks, right after the fair."

Addy threw her arms around Poppa, almost knocking him off his chair. She kissed him on the cheek. "Oh Poppa, Poppa!" she exclaimed. "It's the best news I ever heard!" She sat down on his lap.

Momma said, "You know your poppa been anxious to go. We figure now that we have the garden planted, you and I can take care of it and harvest the vegetables and sell them. We'll need money while Poppa's away and not working. And Poppa's boss say he'll hold Poppa's job for him while he's gone."

"Well, he ain't exactly promise me my job back," Poppa said. "He say if he got work when I get back, he'll take me on again. If not, I'm back where I started, looking for a carpenter job."

"Well, some bosses wouldn't even do that much," Momma said.

Addy was excited by the idea of Poppa going to get Esther, but worries began to fill her mind. Wasn't it dangerous for Poppa to go back to the plantation?

When Master Stevens owned them, he could
do whatever he wanted to them. Wouldn't Master
Stevens be angry at Poppa because she and Momma
had run away? Addy hugged Poppa closer.

"Ain't you scared to go back, Poppa?" she
asked. "Ain't you scared of Master Stevens?"

"He ain't our master no more," Poppa
answered, "and I ain't scared of him."

"But I'm sure he still got guns and whips,
and them mean dogs, too!" Addy said, shivering.

Poppa drew back so Addy could see his face.
"Listen to me," he said. "Slavery is over,

and ain't no man gonna stop me from getting my family."

Addy looked deep into Poppa's dark eyes. They looked calm and peaceful. "Is there anything I can do, Poppa?" she asked. "I'll do anything to help."

"Keep on working in the garden," Poppa said. "Don't let the weeds grow back. And something else, too." He held Addy close in his arms. "Try not to trouble your heart with worry."

"Come on now, Addy," Momma said. "You need to be getting to bed."

Addy gave Momma and Poppa good-night kisses. They stayed at the table talking quietly as Addy said her prayers quickly, dove into bed, and snuggled under her quilt. She held her doll, Ida Bean, close to her. Slowly, slowly, the gentle, peaceful sound of their voices carried her off to sleep.

CHAPTER THREE

HEALING

During the next three weeks, Addy, Momma, and Poppa worked harder than ever in their garden. Addy loved to walk up and down the rows with her watering can and see the little sprouts pushing up out of the earth. She pulled out weeds and kept the soil around the seedlings loose so they had plenty of room to grow.

The day before the fair, Addy and Momma gently dug out some little seedlings Momma was going to sell at the women's booth. They carefully replanted the seedlings in small pots and lined up the pots in a basket.

"I'll bring the basket over to the church," said Addy. "The children's group is meeting there again

34

today. We made our spool puppets and now we gonna paint them."

"All right," said Momma. "But be careful with the seedlings."

"I will," promised Addy.

The basket was heavy, and Addy had to walk slowly. When she got to the church, she went downstairs to the room where the children's group was meeting. She put the basket of seedlings in a sunny corner and sat next to Sarah.

"Oh, look," said Harriet. "Been playing in the dirt again, Addy?"

Addy started to say something sharp, but she bit her lip. Addy really had meant it when she promised Momma and Poppa that she'd try to get along with Harriet. But it was a hard promise to keep. The children's group had met four times to work on the spool puppets and practice the puppet show. Every time, Harriet had been as disagreeable as she could be. Addy could see that today would be no different. She picked up a spool puppet and began to paint it.

"What that puppet going to be?" asked Sarah.

"I think this one gonna be a soldier," answered

Addy. "I'll use the blue paint to make him a uniform."

"A soldier?" snorted Harriet. "That spool puppet will look as much like a soldier as your brother does."

"Don't you talk about my brother that way, Harriet," said Addy.

"Why not?" said Harriet. Her voice was thin and high. "I bet your brother was never a soldier at all. My uncle—"

"Your uncle!" Addy cut in. "We all sick of hearing about your uncle!"

"You're just jealous," snapped Harriet.

"No, I ain't," said Addy, growing more and more angry. "*You* jealous of *me* because everyone liked my idea better than yours."

"How could I be jealous of such a stupid idea?" Harriet scoffed. "That's what these puppets are— stupid!" She threw down the puppet she had been working on, sending the spools scattering across the floor.

"Hey, don't do that!" Sarah yelled. "These puppets ain't stupid. *Yours* might be, but the rest of ours is real good."

"No, they aren't," Harriet yelled back. "We

won't sell a single one! You'll see! We won't make any money and it will all be Addy's fault!"

"If you think they so stupid, then why don't you just leave?" shouted Sarah.

"That's right," said Addy. "We don't need *you*."

Just then Mrs. Drake rushed into the room. "What in heaven's name is going on in here?" she exclaimed. "Who threw this puppet on the floor?"

"Addy started it," Harriet accused.

Addy glared at her. "No, I didn't! You did," she insisted.

"It's all Harriet's fault!" said Sarah.

"Girls!" said Mrs. Drake sternly. "I don't care who started what! I'm surprised at all three of you. You know better than to behave like this, and in church, too! We're supposed to be working for a common purpose here." She looked at the girls and shook her head. "I am going to teach you girls a lesson. The fair is tomorrow. During the morning, I want the three of you to work together at the puppet stage. Just the three of you. I hope that will teach you how to get along. Do you understand me?"

"Yes, ma'am," said Addy, Sarah, and Harriet at the same time.

Harriet turned up her nose and marched back to her seat. Addy sat down next to Sarah and picked up her soldier puppet and paintbrush. But her hands were shaking so from anger that she couldn't hold the brush steady to paint.

That Harriet, she thought. *She got a way of spoiling everything. It's gonna be terrible doing the puppet shows with her! No one can get along with her. She just too mean.*

☀

Addy dreaded working with Harriet so much, she felt as if a rain cloud had cast its gloom over the fair. She was almost surprised to see the sun shining brightly the next morning as she and Momma and Poppa walked to the park where the fair was taking place. When they arrived, Addy couldn't help feeling excited. She had never been to a fair before. She didn't know where to look first.

There were pony rides, horseshoe games, and booths draped with red, white, and blue bunting. People were selling homemade preserves, dough-nuts, and popcorn balls. Soldiers from Camp William Penn were laughing together and trying to win prizes

at the ring toss. Addy could smell fish being fried and chicken being barbecued. Women were setting out loaves of bread and cakes decorated with light clouds of frosting. Nearby, some men were churning ice cream. Addy counted ten freezers! A group of women was slicing lemons and stirring up huge pitchers of lemonade. Addy's mouth was starting to water.

"I'm gonna find Reverend Drake and see what he need me to do," Poppa said. "Now, I know you really here to work, Addy, but take these." He handed Addy three shining pennies. "Don't forget to have a little fun."

"Oh, thank you, Poppa!" Addy said. She knotted the coins in her handkerchief. Three whole cents to spend as she pleased! How would she ever decide what to spend them on?

"Come on over here, Addy," Momma said. "I want to show you where I'm gonna be." She led Addy to a group of booths. In one, women had hung brightly colored quilts they were going to raffle. In others, they had set out pies—cherry, raisin, apple, and sweet potato—to sell.

"Oh, Mrs. Walker," exclaimed a woman at one of the booths. "I'm so sorry! I forgot to bring your seedlings over from the church."

"Momma, I'll run back and get them," offered Addy. "I know where they at."

"All right," said Momma. "You go on and get them, and be careful."

Addy hurried back to the church and ran down the stairs to the Sabbath school room. The seedlings were waiting for her in the sunny corner where she'd left them the day before. Just as she bent over to pick up the basket, she heard a funny sound. It sounded as if someone were crying, and crying hard. Addy put the basket down and looked around. The room was empty. No one was there, and yet she was sure she heard the sound of crying. Addy tiptoed over to the door of the broom closet and opened it slowly. She looked inside and gasped.

There, huddled in a corner, was Harriet. She was crying as if her heart were broken. Her face was hidden in her hands.

"Harriet!" said Addy, surprised. "What . . . what you doing here? What's the matter?"

Harriet didn't answer. She just sobbed.

Addy took a step closer. "You want me to get Mrs. Drake?" she asked. "You sick or something?"

Harriet shook her head, still sobbing.

Addy didn't know what to say. She could hardly believe this was Harriet. Harriet, who was always so haughty!

"Please, Harriet," said Addy. "Tell me what's the matter."

Without lifting her face, Harriet blurted out, "It's my uncle. He's . . . he's dead."

Addy felt as if someone had hit her in the stomach. "What?" she said, shocked. "Your uncle? The one who . . ." She couldn't finish the sentence.

41

Her dislike of Harriet started to drain away. She understood that Harriet was a girl just like she was, whose family had suffered terribly because of the war.

"Oh, Harriet," Addy said with a sigh as she sank to her knees. She reached out her hand and gently touched Harriet's shoulder. "I'm so sorry," she said. "I truly am. I know you loved your uncle. I know you were proud of him."

Harriet lifted her eyes to meet Addy's. "He's dead," she whispered, as if she could not believe it. "I'll never see him again." She hid her face in her hands and cried bitterly.

For a while, Addy just sat there, saying nothing. Finally, when Harriet was crying more softly, Addy said, "I'm sorry if I was mean about him yesterday."

"It doesn't matter," said Harriet. "Nothing matters. I know all of you hate me anyway."

"No, we don't," said Addy. "We don't hate you. Now, you and me ain't tried very hard to get along. We both been hateful and jealous, and I guess we ain't never really gave each other a chance. But it ain't too late to change. I'm sorry. I hope you believe me."

Harriet nodded. She wiped her wet face on the sleeve of her dress. "I . . . I'm sorry, too," she said.

42

"He's dead," Harriet sobbed. "He's dead."

"I was mean to you. I don't blame you for not wanting me around . . ."

"But we *do* want you," said Addy. "We need you. It's just like Reverend Drake said, we got to work together. We got to help each other. I know you feeling bad, but will you come with me to the fair? You might feel better."

When Harriet didn't answer, Addy went on. "Sarah and me can do the puppet show without you if you too shook up to come," she said. "But I sure hope you will come." She looked Harriet in the eye and said kindly, "Nobody else can add up money as quick as you. Will you come and take charge of the money box?"

Harriet took a deep breath. "I'll come," she said.

"Good!" said Addy.

She stood up and led Harriet into the sunny room. When she bent over to pick up the heavy basket of seedlings, Harriet surprised her by lifting one side for her. "Thanks, Harriet. Things sure is easier when somebody's helping you."

Harriet nodded and wiped her eyes. Addy thought she even smiled a little bit.

Addy and Harriet carried the seedlings from the

church to the fair and over to Mrs. Walker's booth.
Then the two girls hurried to the puppet stage.

"Y'all finally here!" exclaimed Sarah. Addy
could tell by the look on her face that Sarah was
surprised to see Addy and Harriet arriving together.
"Come on and get to work. People already been
stopping by. I already sold two puppets
and three slide whistles."

"That's good!" Addy said. "Listen,
Sarah. Harriet don't feel good. She gonna
sell puppets and watch the money box. You
and I can do the puppet show. All right?"

Sarah looked puzzled. She asked, "What's
wrong with her?"

Addy gave Sarah a hard stare and said, "That's
Harriet's business." Then she added softly, "Let's
get started."

Addy and Sarah moved behind the stage, knelt
down next to each other, and pulled a blanket over
their heads.

"What's going on with Harriet?" whispered
Sarah. "Why she acting so quiet?"

"She doing good just to be here," Addy said.
"She just found out her uncle is dead."

"Oh, no!" said Sarah. She shook her head. "That's terrible. She must be feeling real bad."

"She sure is," said Addy.

"I never thought I'd feel sorry for Harriet, but I do," said Sarah.

"Me, too," Addy said.

Suddenly, a voice called from in front of the stage, "Where's the show?"

Addy and Sarah looked at each other. "We better start," said Addy. She took a soldier from the pile of spool puppets and Sarah took a dog. The two girls made their puppets skip across the stage.

Then Addy said in a deep voice, pretending to be the soldier, "Riddle me this. If you found a chicken egg on top of a fence post, how could you tell where it came from?"

Sarah barked like a dog and then said, "I don't know."

"That's easy," Addy made the soldier say. "Chicken eggs come from chickens!"

Addy and Sarah grinned at each other when they heard the people out front laughing. They told a few more riddles and jokes. Then Addy made the puppets dance while Sarah played a song on a slide

The two girls made their puppets skip across the stage.

whistle. When Addy and Sarah came out from behind the stage, they were surprised to see that so many children had gathered. They smiled and bowed while the audience clapped.

Harriet waited until the clapping died down, and then she said, "You can buy the spool puppets and slide whistles here. The puppets cost ten cents each or three for a quarter. The slide whistles cost five cents each."

So many people wanted to buy puppets and whistles that all three girls had to hand them out, collect the money, and make change. By the time they'd finished with the last customer, a new audience had gathered and it was time for Addy and Sarah to put on another show. It was almost two hours before they had time to take a break.

"You were right, Addy," said Harriet. She was buying herself a slide whistle. "I can't believe how well the puppets and whistles are selling."

"We gonna sell them all!" Sarah said confidently. "Hey, everybody," she called out. "Come right on over to our booth and buy our puppets and whistles. They going fast!"

The three girls laughed together at Sarah's

clowning, but not for long. Quickly, another crowd gathered and they had to go back to work.

Just before the last show of the morning, Mrs. Drake came to the puppet stage. "Well, I see you girls are getting along well," she said happily, "and your puppet shows are the hit of the fair. Everyone is enjoying them. Every child I see seems to be wearing one of the slide whistles around his neck."

"We sure have sold a lot of puppets and whistles," said Harriet. "I already counted the money. We've made nearly seven dollars."

"That's wonderful," Mrs. Drake said.

"Do you want to collect the money?" Addy asked.

"Not yet," said Mrs. Drake. "I'll come back in a while."

"Don't wait too long," Sarah joked, "or the money box gonna overflow!"

As Mrs. Drake and the girls laughed, Addy noticed a tall older girl standing at the puppet stage. She was wearing a blue dress with a blue sash. Her dress was nice, so Addy was surprised that she was carrying a big, dirty carpetbag. The girl put the bag on the ground next to the puppet stage while she picked up puppets, inspected them, and put them down.

"Hello," Addy said to the older girl. "Do you want to buy a puppet?"

"I'm just looking," said the girl sharply. "It's not against the law to look, is it?"

"No, of course it ain't," said Addy.

Just then, a large group of children arrived at the puppet stage. Addy and Sarah put on a show for the children while Harriet sold more puppets and whistles. After the children left, when Addy was selling a puppet to a soldier, she saw the older girl still lingering near the puppet stage. Then she seemed to vanish into the crowd. When Addy turned to put the soldier's money in the money box, she couldn't find the box. She looked on the ground behind the stage, beneath the box of puppets, and next to the box of slide whistles.

"What you looking for?" asked Sarah.

"The money box," Addy said in a worried voice. "Where is it?"

"Isn't it behind the stage?" asked Harriet.

"No, it ain't!" exclaimed Sarah, looking around frantically. "It's gone!"

"Oh, no!" groaned Harriet. "All our money! Somebody must have stolen it."

Suddenly, Addy knew exactly what had happened.

"It was that tall girl!" she said quickly. "The one with the bag! I just know she's the one who stole the money. Sarah, go tell Reverend Drake. Come on, Harriet! Let's catch her!"

CHAPTER
FOUR
—

ALL FOR ONE

 Addy and Harriet ran as fast as they
could through the crowded fair. Past
the women's booths, past the pony
rides, past the games they ran, nearly colliding with
a group of soldiers who were pitching horseshoes.
Addy's heart was beating very fast. She kept
running and searching all around her for the girl
with the carpetbag.

"Addy!" she heard Harriet gasp behind her.
"I can't keep up with you."

Addy stopped and turned. "Let's split up," she
panted. "We both got whistles. Blow yours three
times if you see the girl, and I'll do the same."

Harriet nodded, and Addy ran off again. Addy

thought about trying to find Mrs. Drake and ask for help, but she decided that would waste time. She had to keep running. Suddenly, up ahead of her, Addy saw a group of girls walking along. One girl wore a blue dress! Addy tore over to the girls, ready to blow her whistle to call Harriet. But when Addy tapped the girl in the blue dress on the arm and the girl turned around, she realized it wasn't the one who had been at the puppet stage.

"Sorry," Addy said breathlessly. "I thought you was somebody else."

She paused for a moment, unsure where to run next. She felt desperate. The older girl could be far away by now. Addy was about to take off running again when she heard a whistle blowing. One, two, three times. One, two, three times. *It's Harriet,* Addy thought. *She found the girl!*

Addy ran toward the sound of the whistle. Out of the corner of her eye, Addy saw the girl running past the women's booths, clutching the carpetbag close to her. Harriet was right behind her.

Addy joined in the chase, her arms and legs pumping hard, her heart pounding, and her whistle bouncing against her chest. Harriet was closing in

fast on the girl, when suddenly, *slam!* The older
girl turned and swung the bag with all her might,
knocking Harriet down with a sickening thud.

Addy heard Harriet cry out in pain. Addy raced
to see if she was hurt, but Harriet yelled, "Go, Addy!
Don't let her get away!" Two women rushed to
Harriet to help her, so Addy continued the chase.

"Stop that girl!" Addy yelled, pointing at the tall
girl. "Stop her! She's a thief!"

The girl made a quick turn past the food booths.
Addy took a shortcut, jumping over the row of ice
cream freezers. She caught up with the girl as she
came streaking past the freezers. Addy reached out,
grabbed the handle of the carpetbag, and held on
with all her strength. Just at that moment, Reverend
Drake and two other men rushed toward Addy and
the girl. The tall girl let go of the bag, sending Addy
crashing to the ground. Then the girl took off,
disappearing into the crowd.

Addy was still holding on to the handle of the
carpetbag for all she was worth when Reverend
Drake helped her stand up. "Are you all right,
Addy?" he asked.

Sarah and Harriet pushed through the crowd

*Addy reached out, grabbed the handle of the carpetbag,
and held on with all her strength.*

in time to hear Addy answer, "I'm fine, Reverend." Her dress was torn at the hem and one knee was bruised, but no serious harm was done. The three girls smiled at one another.

"I'm glad that girl ain't hurt y'all," said Sarah. "And I'm glad you got the bag, Addy!"

Harriet didn't say anything, but she reached out and gave Addy a quick hug.

"Sarah told me about the theft," said Reverend Drake. "We've been following you, but you were running so fast, we couldn't catch up with you."

"I had to catch her," Addy explained, still out of breath. "I couldn't let her get away with the money, not after we worked so hard." With great relief, Addy handed the carpetbag to Reverend Drake. "I think the money box is in here," she said.

Reverend Drake opened the carpetbag. Everyone in the crowd gasped when he pulled out *three* money boxes. "Why, there must be fifty dollars in these boxes," said Reverend Drake. "If you girls hadn't stopped her, there's no telling how many boxes she could have taken."

"It was really Addy who saved the day," said Harriet, "with her quick thinking."

"And her quick running," added Sarah.

"No," Addy said. "It was all of us working together. None of us could have caught her alone."

"I'm grateful to all three of you girls," said Reverend Drake. "I guess you're probably tired out. The other children can take over the puppet stage now."

"Oh, no, thank you," said Addy. "We ain't tired. We need to be getting back to our stage so we can do one last show."

"That's right," said Harriet with a happy look at Addy. "It's easy when we help each other."

"All right then," said Reverend Drake. "I'll come with you. I've been wanting to see one of your shows all morning."

When they got back to the puppet stage, Addy and Sarah took their places behind the stage and pulled the blanket over themselves.  Addy picked up the soldier puppet again, and Sarah found her dog puppet.

"Riddle me this," Addy made the soldier ask the dog. "What's smaller than you, but can put a bear on the run?"

"A cat?" Sarah had the dog puppet answer.

"No, no, no, silly," said the soldier puppet.

Suddenly someone in the audience spoke out in a deep voice, "That's an easy riddle. Even my little sister know that one. It's a skunk."

Addy's heart stopped still. She threw off the blanket, popped up from behind the stage, and looked straight into the face of a soldier who looked just like Poppa. But it wasn't Poppa.

"Addy!" the soldier cried.

"Sam?" gasped Addy, not trusting her eyes. "Sam! It *is* you!" She ran out from behind the booth and threw her arms around him. Sarah, Harriet, and Reverend Drake watched.

"Oh, Sam! I can't hardly believe you're here!" said Addy. She pulled back to get a good look at Sam, and it was then she realized that Sam was missing an arm. Gently, Addy touched the empty sleeve that was pinned to his shoulder and then turned a sad face up to Sam.

"Don't cry," Sam said. His voice was much deeper than it had been the last time Addy had seen him. "I'm fine. I lost my arm in a battle, but I'm here. I'm telling you, I'm lucky to be here. I just got to

Philadelphia yesterday. And now everything gonna be all right, Addy. Now that I found you, everything gonna be all right."

Addy laughed and smiled up at her brother through the tears in her eyes. "*You* found *me?*" she teased. "We been looking for you so long, Sam—" She stopped and gave Sam another hug, too happy to talk.

"Come on," she finally said. "Let's go find Momma and Poppa."

Addy skipped next to Sam as if she were in a happy dream.

"Riddle me this, Sam," she said. "What holds a family together so tight that nothing can pull it apart?"

"I give up," said Sam with a smile.

"It's easy," said Addy, looking up at her brother with pride. "It's love."

**LOOKING
BACK
1864**

A PEEK INTO
THE PAST

A painting of New York City's Central Park done in Addy's time.

When Addy was growing up, American cities were growing, too. Immigrants from many countries poured into American cities. During and after the Civil War, many formerly enslaved people, like Addy's family, moved to cities from farms and plantations. Other people, too, left their farms to move into cities.

All the new people in cities needed places to live, but housing was expensive and hard to find. Many families, like Addy's, shared one or two rooms. Boarding houses and apartment buildings were often squeezed together, with alleys behind them instead of backyards. Sanitation was poor in the 1860s. In many cities, garbage and sewage were dumped into the same rivers that drinking water came from. Factory smokestacks poured dirty black smoke into the air.

Factories like this one in Chicago sent clouds of black smoke into the air.

Many wealthy people left the crowds, smells, and noises of the city in the summer. They traveled to resorts to cool off. Poor and working-class people who could not afford such trips went to public parks to relax and be outdoors. Families, church groups, and many clubs and other organizations had picnics, barbecues, and festivals in city parks. In

many public places in Philadelphia and other cities, African Americans had to use separate areas from whites, but usually everyone could enjoy the public parks freely.

Before the Civil War, public parks were usually very small squares of open land. But by the 1850s, people wanted cities to have large parks with acres

Children playing in a city park.

of meadows, tree-lined paths, and ponds. They believed that everyone, rich and poor, could enjoy nature in these

63

larger parks. Being close to nature would create feelings of happiness. Some people even believed that visits to parks for fresh air and sunshine could prevent diseases such as cholera and typhoid fever, which killed thousands of people each year.

In the late 1850s, Americans began to build large parks right in the middle of cities. The first such park was Central Park in New York City. Other cities soon

A bird's-eye view of New York City's Central Park in the 1860s.

followed, including Philadelphia, which built the first public zoo in the United States in Fairmount Park. People in Philadelphia and New York still use these parks today. Some trees planted right after the Civil War are still standing in these parks.

This memorial to the Civil War soldier still stands in New Hampshire today.

People wanted statues and monuments in their new parks, too. Before the 1860s, many cities had put up statues of such national heroes as Benjamin Franklin and George Washington. At the end of the Civil War, new monuments were planned for President Abraham Lincoln as well as for important generals and admirals who had fought in the war. But for the first time, the public also wanted to build statues to honor the ordinary young soldiers who had fought and died for their country. For many years, only white soldiers were represented by these statues, even though black men fought in the Civil War, too.

A detail from a memorial to black soldiers who fought in the Civil War. It was put up in Boston in the 1890s.

City children sometimes played in parks. More often, they played on sidewalks, in alleys, and in empty lots near their homes because children's playgrounds were rare in Addy's time. City people also could go swimming in the hot summer months if there was a river or lake nearby. But

65

A woman's swimsuit from Addy's time.

before the 1860s, girls and women didn't go swimming very often. It was thought improper for them to swim with boys and men, and their swimsuits were like bulky dresses that covered the entire body. A few large cities built bathing houses where men and women could swim separately indoors.

By the middle of the 1800s, city people were starting to enjoy watching sports. Large crowds of people gathered to watch track and field races and boxing, cricket, and rowing competitions. Baseball became an especially popular sport during and just after the Civil War. Baseball teams were formed in large cities, and the teams traveled by railroad to games in other cities. But in the 1860s, baseball teams were *segregated*. This meant

Children playing baseball outside a public school for black students in New York.

A baseball from the 1860s.

that no black person could play on a team with white players. Philadelphia's black community formed its own baseball team, the Pythians, who played against other teams of African-American players.

When the Civil War ended, Americans began recovering from years of wartime hardship and suffering. Many Americans who had been living in slavery began looking for loved ones who were separated from them during or before the war. Families like Addy's worked long hours to make new lives for themselves. Vacations were not possible, but most Americans, even city residents, found ways to relax and have fun outdoors during the summer months.

Newly freed people started to make new lives for themselves in the city.